Muledred

by **Kathryn Brown**

Harcourt Brace Jovanovich, Publishers

San Diego   New York   London

Requests for permission to make copies of any part of the work
should be mailed to: Permissions Department,
Harcourt Brace Jovanovich, Publishers, Orlando, Florida 32887.

Library of Congress Cataloging-in-Publication Data
Brown, Kathryn, 1955–
Muledred / written and illustrated by Kathryn Brown. — 1st ed.   p.   cm.
Summary: With the help of her grandfather's watch, Muledred
the mule finally gets to school on time.
ISBN 0-15-256265-6
[1. Mules — Fiction. 2. Tardiness — Fiction. 3. Clocks
and watches — Fiction.] I. Title.
PZ7.B81554Mu   1990   [E] — dc20   89-11027

First edition   A B C D E

For J O E Y

The illustrations in this book were done in watercolor
and pencil on Waterford watercolor paper.
The display type was hand-lettered by Judythe Sieck.
The text type was set in ITC Garamond Light
by Thompson Type, San Diego, California.
Color separations were made by Bright Arts, Ltd., Hong Kong.
Printed and bound by Tien Wah Press, Singapore
Production supervision by Warren Wallerstein and Michele Green
Edited by Jane Yolen and designed by Camilla Filancia

Muledred was always late for school. Each time she was late, Master Skinner made her stay after.

One day, her grandpa gave her his pocket watch, the very one he used for work.

"This will get you to school on time," he told her, "as long as you remember to check it. But it is very old. It loses time. Every morning it needs to be set ahead five minutes. Don't forget."

The next morning, Muledred and her friend Alfred left for school. But she forgot to set the watch ahead.

Along the way they stopped at the pear tree. Muledred glanced at the watch and said, "We have lots of time. We can pick pears. We can even bring Master Skinner one."

They picked three pears each. Then they got on their bikes and rode.

They came to the wishing well.

"Let's stop and look for frogs," Muledred said.
"We still have lots of time."

"I don't think we do," said Alfred. "C'mon, Muledred."
He rode off.

But Muledred stopped. She peeked in the wishing
well. Then, remembering to check the time, she reached
into her pocket for the watch. It was gone!

"Oh, no!" she thought. "Maybe I lost it at the pear tree."

She started back but heard the school bell ring.

"Whoa!" she shouted. "I'll have to look later." She tried to turn around too fast.

Whiz!

Wham!

Bang!

Splat!

She crashed her bike.

Alfred arrived on time,

but where was Muledred?

"Late again," said Master Skinner when Muledred finally arrived.

"But I lost my watch," Muledred tried to explain. "I think it's at the pear tree."

Master Skinner would not listen to her excuses.
She was twenty minutes late, so she had to stay twenty
minutes after school.

Alfred waited for her outside.

Afterward they trudged home, Muledred pushing her broken bike. So she wouldn't be too sad, Alfred pushed his bike, too. They looked for her watch along the way.

"We'll surely find it at the pear tree," Alfred told her.

Instead they found Levi and Amos waiting under the tree, eating pears.

"Muledred Mule was late for school!" Levi and Amos teased. *"Again!"*

Muledred was annoyed. "You two think you're so important just because you ring the bell every morning. Why can't you ever wait for me to get there?"

"Muledred Mule, we can't wait. We must ring the bell at eight."

"Then *don't* wait," Muledred said angrily. "Because tomorrow I'll ring the bell first."

"Hee-haw! Hee-haw! Hee-haw!" they laughed.

Levi looked at her bike and snickered. "You won't get there on that bike. But I'll tell you what — if you're there on time tomorrow, this watch I just found is yours."

Muledred gasped. "That *is* mine! Give it back."

"Only if you're on time," said Levi, and he snatched the watch away.

"Yeah," piped in Amos. "Finders keepers, losers weepers. Hee-haw! Hee-haw! Hee-haw!"

Muledred and Alfred went to her grandpa's. They left her bike to be fixed.

"I need it bright and early, Grandpa," Muledred said.

"I'll try," Grandpa replied.

"I can pick you up tomorrow," offered Alfred. Then he gave her a ride home on the back of his bike.

The next morning Muledred was ready at daybreak.
"Oh, my," said her mother. "You're early, Muledred.
But Alfred is even earlier."

Alfred had bad news. "I'm sorry, Muledred. My
brother is sick. I have to do his paper route. I can't ride
you to your grandpa's after all. But you'll still have plenty
of time."

Muledred ran all the way.

More bad news. The bike needed a new wheel.

"Oh, no, Grandpa," Muledred cried. "What am I going to do?"

"You're just going to have to hoof it," said Grandpa.

"But I've got to get to school early today," she said.

"It's early *now*," said Grandpa. "Look at the watch."

Muledred gulped. Now she would have to tell him.

"I lost the watch, Grandpa. Levi and Amos found it.
They said I could have it back if I get to school in time
to ring the bell today."

Grandpa wiped away her tears with his handkerchief. "Well, it's not too late to get it back, Muledred. All you have to do is go straight there. Don't get sidetracked. Don't daydream. Just one hoof in front of the other."

Muledred trotted off as fast as she could.

Clippity, clippity, clippity clop. She passed by the pear tree. Clippity, clippity, clippity clop.

Alfred caught up with her at the wishing well.

"Hop on, Muledred," he hollered, "You're sure going to be early today!"

They sped around the bend and up the last hill. They didn't stop until they came into the schoolyard. They were the first ones there except for Master Skinner, who was just opening the schoolhouse door.

Muledred ran to the bell. Master Skinner checked the clock and nodded at her. She pulled the rope hard. It was the loudest ring she had ever heard.

Soon the class began to gather.

Far down the hill Muledred could see Levi and Amos. They were running as fast as they could, but they were going to be late.

When they finally got to class, huffing and puffing, Levi and Amos looked at Muledred.

"You can have your old watch," they said. "It doesn't work right anyway."

Muledred took her grandpa's watch.

"That's funny," she said, "it got *me* to school on time."

She wrote on her slate: "Five minutes plus five minutes equals ten minutes late."

Carefully she set the old watch ahead ten minutes and slipped it into her pocket. She winked at Alfred. "They're going to have to stay ten minutes after school."

Alfred laughed. "Hee-haw! Hee-haw! Hee-haw!"